Listen,
My Children

POEMS FOR SECOND GRADERS

A CORE KNOWLEDGE® BOOK

LISTEN, MY CHILDREN: POEMS FOR SECOND GRADERS
ONE IN A SERIES, *POEMS FOR KINDERGARTNERS—FIFTH GRADERS*,
COLLECTING THE POEMS IN THE *CORE KNOWLEDGE SEQUENCE*

A CORE KNOWLEDGE® BOOK

SERIES EDITOR: SUSAN TYLER HITCHCOCK
RESEARCHER: JEANNE NICHOLSON SILER
EDITORIAL ASSISTANT: KRISTEN D. MOSES
CONSULTANT: STEPHEN B. CUSHMAN
GENERAL EDITOR: E. D. HIRSCH JR.

LIBRARY OF CONGRESS CARD CATALOG NUMBER: 00-111615

ISBN 10: 1-890517-30-5

ISBN 13: 978-1890517-30-4

PRINTED IN CANADA
DESIGN BY DIANE NELSON GRAPHIC DESIGN
COVER ART COPYRIGHT © BY LANCE HIDY, LANCE@LANCEHIDY.COM

CORE KNOWLEDGE FOUNDATION
801 EAST HIGH STREET
CHARLOTTESVILLE, VIRGINIA 22902
WWW.COREKNOWLEDGE.ORG

About this Book

"LISTEN, MY CHILDREN, and you shall hear . . ." So begins a famous poem about Paul Revere, written by Henry Wadsworth Longfellow in 1855. This opening line reminds us that every time we read a poem, we hear that poem as well. The sounds and rhythms of the words are part of the poem's meaning. Poems are best understood when read out loud, or when a reader hears the sounds of the words in his or her head while reading silently.

This six-volume series collects all the poems in the Core Knowledge Sequence for kindergarten through fifth grade. Each volume includes occasional notes about the poems and biographical sketches about the poets' authors, but the focus is really the poems themselves. Some have been chosen because they reflect times past; others because of their literary fame; still others were selected because they express states of mind shared by many children.

This selection of poetry, part of the *Core Knowledge Sequence*, is based on the work of E. D. Hirsch Jr., author of *Cultural Literacy* and *The Schools We Need*. The Sequence outlines a core curriculum for preschool through grade eight in English and language arts, history and geography, math, science, fine art, and music. It is designed to ensure that children are exposed to the essential knowledge that establishes cultural literacy as they also acquire a broad, firm foundation for higher-level schooling. Its first version was developed in 1990 at a convention of teachers and subject matter experts. Revised in 1995 to reflect the classroom experience of Core Knowledge teachers, the Sequence is now used in hundreds of schools across America. Its content also guides the Core Knowledge Series, *What Your Kindergartner—Sixth Grader Needs to Know*.

Contents

Who Has Seen the Wind?

by Christina Rossetti

Who has seen the wind?
   Neither I nor you:
But when the leaves hang trembling,
   The wind is passing through.

Who has seen the wind?
   Neither you nor I:
But when the leaves bow down their heads,
   The wind is passing by.

Windy Nights

by Robert Louis Stevenson

Whenever the moon and stars are set,
　　Whenever the wind is high,
All night long in the dark and wet,
　　A man goes riding by,
Late in the night when fires are out,
Why does he gallop and gallop about?

Whenever the trees are crying aloud,
　　And ships are tossed at sea,
By, on the highway, low and loud,
　　By at the gallop goes he.
By at the gallop he goes, and then
By he comes back at the gallop again.

Robert Louis Stevenson
1850–1894

As a boy, Robert Louis Stevenson was often ill. Still he wrote *A Child's Garden of Verses,* one of the most famous books of poems about the pleasures of being a child. He wrote other books, too, including the novels *Treasure Island* and *Kidnapped.* As he grew older, he became ill again. He and his wife moved to the island of Samoa, in the South Pacific, where he was called Tusitala, "Teller of Tales."

Something Told the Wild Geese

by Rachel Field

Something told the wild geese
It was time to go.
Though the fields lay golden
Something whispered — "Snow."
Leaves were green and stirring,
Berries, luster-glossed,
But beneath warm feathers
Something cautioned — "Frost."
All the sagging orchards
Steamed with amber spice,
But each wild breast stiffened
At remembered ice.
Something told the wild geese
It was time to fly —
Summer sun was on their wings,
Winter in their cry.

Caterpillars

by Aileen Fisher

What do caterpillars do?
Nothing much but chew and chew.

What do caterpillars know?
Nothing much but how to grow.

They just eat what by and by
will make them be a butterfly,

But that is more than I can do
however much I chew and chew.

Bee! I'm Expecting You!

by Emily Dickinson

Bee! I'm expecting you!
Was saying Yesterday
To Somebody you know
That you were due —

The Frogs got Home last Week —
Are settled, and at work —
Birds, mostly back —
The Clover warm and thick —

You'll get my Letter by
The Seventeenth; Reply
Or better, be with me —
Yours, Fly

Emily Dickinson
1830–1886

Almost all of Emily Dickinson's life was spent in the little town of Amherst, Massachusetts. No one knew that she wrote poems. After she died, her sister found her poems hidden in a dresser drawer.

Seashell

by Federico Garcia Lorca
translated by K. F. Pearson

They've brought me a seashell.

Inside it sings
a map of the sea.
My heart
fills up with water,
with smallish fish
of shade and silver.

They've brought me a seashell.

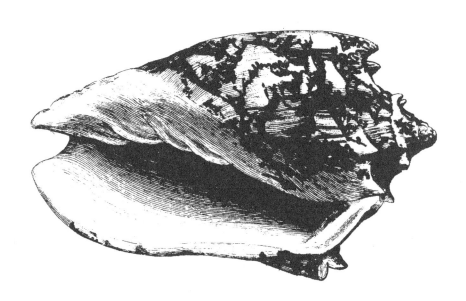

Discovery

by Harry Behn

In a puddle left from last week's rain,
    A friend of mine whose name is Joe
    Caught a tadpole, and showed me where
    Its froggy legs were beginning to grow.

Then we turned over a musty log,
    With lichens on it in a row,
    And found some fiddleheads of ferns
    Uncoiling out of the moss below.

We hunted around, and saw the first
    Jack-in-the-pulpits beginning to show,
    And even discovered under a rock
    Where spotted salamanders go.

    I learned all this one morning from Joe,
    But how much more there is to know!

MUSTY
Wet and moldy.

LICHENS
[LIE-kens]
Crusty, funguslik
plants that grow
on wood and
rock.

JACK-IN-THE-PULPITS
Spring
wildflowers.

Hurt No Living Thing

by Christina Rossetti

Hurt no living thing;
Ladybird, nor butterfly,
Nor moth with dusty wing,
Nor cricket chirping cheerily,
Nor grasshopper so light of leap,
Nor dancing gnat, nor beetle fat,
Nor harmless worms that creep.

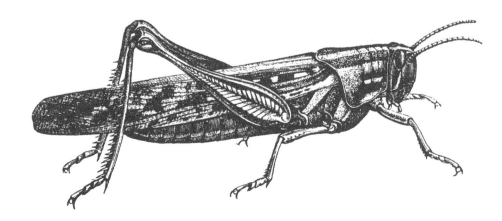

Bed in Summer

by Robert Louis Stevenson

In winter I get up at night
And dress by yellow candle-light.
In summer, quite the other way,
I have to go to bed by day.

I have to go to bed and see
The birds still hopping on the tree,
Or hear the grown-up people's feet
Still going past me in the street.

And does it not seem hard to you,
When all the sky is clear and blue,
And I should like so much to play,
To have to go to bed by day?

Since Robert Louis Stevenson lived in the 19th century, before wires brought electricity to houses, his family would have lit oil lamps and candles for light.

Carl Sandburg
1878–1967

Carl Sandburg's parents came to the United States from Sweden. When he grew up, he wrote poems to celebrate the United States and its people. He chose simple words and phrases, so many people could read his poems. He also wrote a famous biography of Abraham Lincoln.

Buffalo Dusk

by Carl Sandburg

The buffaloes are gone.

And those who saw the buffaloes are gone.

Those who saw the buffaloes by thousands and how they

pawed the prairie sod into dust with their hoofs, their great

heads down pawing on in a great pageant of dusk,

Those who saw the buffaloes are gone.

And the buffaloes are gone.

PAGEANT
A grand
display or
show

Gwendolyn Brooks
1917–2000

Gwendolyn Brooks was born in Kansas, but she grew up in the city of Chicago. In 1950 she received the Pulitzer Prize for Poetry. She was the first African American to win this important prize.

Rudolph Is Tired of the City

by Gwendolyn Brooks

These buildings are too close to me.
I'd like to PUSH away.
I'd like to live in the country,
And spread my arms all day.

I'd like to spread my breath out, too —
As farmers' sons and daughters do.

I'd tend the cows and chickens.
I'd do the other chores.
Then, all the hours left I'd go
A-SPREADING out-of-doors.

Harriet Tubman

by Eloise Greenfield

Harriet Tubman didn't take no stuff
Wasn't scared of nothing neither
Didn't come in this world to be no slave
And wasn't going to stay one either

"Farewell!" she sang to her friends one night
She was mighty sad to leave 'em
But she ran away that dark, hot night
Ran looking for her freedom

She ran to the woods and she ran through the woods
With the slave catchers right behind her
And she kept on going till she got to the North
Where those mean men couldn't find her

Nineteen times she went back South
To get three hundred others
She ran for her freedom nineteen times
To save Black sisters and brothers

Harriet Tubman didn't take no stuff
Wasn't scared of nothing neither
Didn't come in this world to be no slave
And didn't stay one either

And didn't stay one either

Harriet Tubman was a slave who escaped in 1849 and then worked to free other slaves. She helped form the "Underground Railroad," which was a secret network of people who protected slaves as they ran away from plantations and traveled to states where they could escape slavery.

Lincoln

by Nancy Byrd Turner

There was a boy of other days,
A quiet, awkward, earnest lad,
Who trudged long weary miles to get
A book on which his heart was set —
And then no candle had!

He was too poor to buy a lamp
But very wise in woodmen's ways.
He gathered seasoned bough and stem,
And crisping leaf, and kindled them
Into a ruddy blaze.

Then as he lay full length and read,
The firelight flickered on his face,
And etched his shadow on the gloom,
And made a picture in the room,
In that most humble place.

The hard years came, the hard years went,
But, gentle, brave, and strong of will,
He met them all. And when today
We see his pictured face, we say,
"There's light upon it still."

There Was an Old Man with a Beard

by Edward Lear

There was an old man with a beard,
Who said, "It is just as I feared!
    Two Owls and a Hen,
    Four Larks and a Wren,
Have all built their nests in my beard!"

This poem is a "limerick." Limericks always have five lines that follow the same rhythm and rhyme scheme, and they usually tell a joke. It's fun to write your own limericks.

Smart

by Shel Silverstein

My dad gave me one dollar bill
'Cause I'm his smartest son,
And I swapped it for two shiny quarters
'Cause two is more than one!

And then I took the quarters
And traded them to Lou
For three dimes — I guess he don't know
That three is more than two!

Just then, along came old blind Bates
And just 'cause he can't see
He gave me four nickels for my three dimes,
And four is more than three!

And I took the nickels to Hiram Coombs
Down at the seed-feed store,
And the fool gave me five pennies for them,
And five is more than four!

And then I went and showed my dad,
And he got red in the cheeks
And closed his eyes and shook his head —
Too proud of me to speak!

The Night Before Christmas

by Clement C. Moore

'Twas the night before Christmas,

When all through the house

Not a creature was stirring, not even a mouse.

The stockings were hung by the chimney with care,

In hopes that St. Nicholas soon would be there.

The children were nestled all snug in their beds,

While visions of sugar-plums danced in their heads.

And Mama in her kerchief, and I in my cap

Had just settled down for a long winter's nap,

When out on the lawn there arose such a clatter,

That I sprang from my bed to see what was the matter.

Away to the window I flew like a flash,

Tore open the shutters and threw up the sash.

The moon on the breast of the new fallen snow,

Gave the luster of mid-day to objects below.

When what to my wondering eyes should appear,

But a miniature sleigh and eight tiny reindeer

With a little old driver so lively and quick

I knew in a moment it must be St. Nick.

More rapid than eagles his coursers they came,

And he whistled, and shouted, and called them by name:

"Now, Dasher! Now, Dancer! Now, Prancer and Vixen!

On, Comet! On, Cupid! On Donder and Blitzen!

To the top of the porch! To the top of the wall!

Now dash away! Dash away! Dash away all!"

As dry leaves that before the wild hurricane fly,
When they meet with an obstacle, mount to the sky,
So up to the housetop the coursers they flew,
With a sleigh full of toys and St. Nicholas, too.
And then, in a twinkling, I heard on the roof
The prancing and pawing of each little hoof.
As I drew in my head and was turning around . . .
Down the chimney St. Nicholas came with a bound!
He was dressed all in fur from his head to his foot,
And his clothes were all tarnished with ashes and soot;
A bundle of toys he had flung on his back,
And he looked like a pedlar just opening his pack.

His eyes — how they twinkled, his dimples how merry!
His cheeks were like roses, his nose like a cherry!
His droll little mouth was drawn like a bow,
And the beard on his chin was as white as the snow.
The stump of a pipe he held tight in his teeth,
And the smoke it encircled his head like a wreath.
He had a broad face and a round little belly,
That shook when he laughed like a bowlful of jelly.
He was chubby and plump. A right jolly old elf,
And I laughed when I saw him in spite of myself!
A wink of his eye and a twist of his head
Soon gave me to know I had nothing to dread.
He spoke not a word, but went straight to his work,
And fill'd all the stockings — then turned with a jerk . . .
And laying his finger aside his nose,
And giving a nod, up the chimney he rose!
He sprang to his sleigh, to his team gave a whistle,
And away they all flew like the down of a thistle.
But I heard him exclaim, 'ere he drove out of sight . . .
"Happy Christmas to all, and to all a good night!"

The Wind

by Robert Louis Stevenson

I saw you toss the kites on high,
And blow the birds about the sky;
And all around I heard you pass,
Like ladies' skirts across the grass —
    O wind, a-blowing all day long,
    O wind, that sings so loud a song!

I saw the different things you did,
But always you yourself you hid.
I felt you push, I heard you call,
I could not see yourself at all —
    O wind, a-blowing all day long,
    O wind, that sings so loud a song!

O you that are so strong and cold,
O blower, are you young or old?
Are you a beast of field and tree,
Or just a stronger child than me?
    O wind, a-blowing all day long,
    O wind, that sings so loud a song!

Where Go the Boats?

by Robert Louis Stevenson

Dark brown is the river,
    Golden is the sand.
It flows along for ever,
    With trees on either hand.

Green leaves a-floating,
    Castles of the foam,
Boats of mine a-boating —
    Where will all come home?

On goes the river
    And out past the mill,
Away down the valley,
    Away down the hill.

Away down the river,
    A hundred miles or more,
Other little children
    Shall bring my boats ashore.

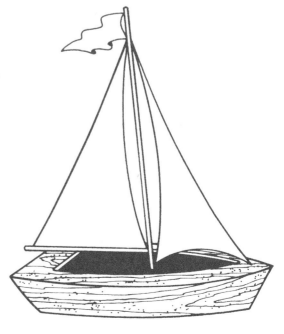

The Duel

by Eugene Field

The gingham dog and the calico cat
Side by side on the table sat;
'Twas half-past twelve, and (what do you think!)
Nor one nor t' other had slept a wink!
    The old Dutch clock and the Chinese plate
    Appeared to know as sure as fate
There was going to be a terrible spat.

    (I wasn't there; I simply state
    What was told to me by the Chinese plate!)

The gingham dog went "bow-wow-wow!"
And the calico cat replied "mee-ow!"
The air was littered, an hour or so,
With bits of gingham and calico,
    While the old Dutch clock in the chimney-place
    Up with its hands before its face,
For it always dreaded a family row!

    (Now mind: I'm only telling you
    What the old Dutch clock declares is true!)

GINGHAM, CALICO
Fabric used to make quilts.

A FAMILY ROW
A family argument.

The Chinese plate looked very blue,
And wailed, "Oh, dear! what shall we do!"
But the gingham dog and the calico cat
Wallowed this way and tumbled that,
　　Employing every tooth and claw
　　In the awfullest way you ever saw —
And, oh! how the gingham and calico flew!

　　(Don't fancy I exaggerate —
　　I got my news from the Chinese plate!)

Next morning, where the two had sat
They found no trace of dog or cat;
And some folks think unto this day
That burglars stole that pair away!
　　But the truth about the cat and pup
　　Is this: they ate each other up!
Now what do you really think of that!

　　(The old Dutch clock it told me so,
　　And that is how I came to know.)

Acknowledgments

Every care has been taken to trace and acknowledge copyright of the poems and images in this volume. If accidental infringement has occurred, the editor offers apologies and welcomes communications that allow proper acknowledgment in subsequent editions.

"Something Told the Wild Geese" from *Poems* by Rachel Field. Copyright © 1934 Macmillan Publishing Company; copyright renewed © 1962 by Arthur S. Pederson. Reprinted with the permission of Simon & Schuster Books for Young Readers, an imprint of Simon & Schuster Children's Publishing Division.

"Caterpillars" from *Cricket in a Thicket* by Aileen Fisher. Copyright © 1963, 1991 Aileen Fisher. Used by permission of Marian Reiner for the author.

"Bee! I'm Expecting You!" from *The Poems of Emily Dickinson*, Thomas H. Johnson, ed., Cambridge, Mass: The Belknap Press of Harvard University Press. Copyright © 1951, 1955, 1979 by the President and Fellows of Harvard College. Reprinted by permission of the publishers and the Trustees of Amherst College.

"Seashell" by Federico Garcia Lorca, from *Messages of Things*, by K. F. Pearson. Copyright © 1984 by K. F. Pearson.

"Discovery" from *Crickets and Bullfrogs and Whispers of Thunder, Poems and Pictures* by Harry Behn. Copyright © 1957, 1962, 1966 by Harry Behn. All rights renewed. Used by permission of Marian Reiner.

"Buffalo Dusk" from *Smoke and Steel* by Carl Sandburg. Copyright © 1920 by Harcourt, Inc., renewed 1948 by Carl Sandburg. Reprinted by permission of Harcourt, Inc.

"Rudolph is Tired of the City" from *Bronzeville Boys and Girls* by Gwendolyn Brooks. Copyright © 1956 by Gwendolyn Brooks Blakely. Used by permission of HarperCollins Publishers.

"Harriet Tubman" from *Honey, I Love*, by Eloise Greenfield. Copyright © 1978 by Eloise Greenfield. Used by permission of HarperCollins Publishers.

"Smart" from *Where the Sidewalk Ends*, by Shel Silverstein. Copyright © 1974 by Evil Eye Music, Inc. Selection reprinted by permission of HarperCollins Publishers.

Images:
Robert Louis Stevenson: © Bettmann/CORBIS
Emily Dickinson: By permission of Amherst College Archives and Special Collections
Carl Sandburg: © Bettmann/CORBIS
Gwendolyn Brooks: © Bettmann/CORBIS